THE HIGHEST PRAISE FOR
MILDRED D. TAYLOR'S

THE FRIENDSHIP

"A powerful story, there is no doubt. Readers will be haunted by its drama and emotion long after they have closed the book. . . . Ginsburg's pen-and-ink drawings are excellent, adding much to the intensity of the narrative."   —*Booklist*

"From its quiet beginning, the tension grows relentlessly in this brief, carefully designed story. . . . Ginsburg's black-and-white drawings are outstanding."   —*Kirkus Reviews*

"The social drama elicits a naturally powerful response in depicting cruel injustice, and the writing is concentrated to heighten that effect."
—Bulletin of the Center for Children's Books

AND

THE GOLD CADILLAC

"Mildred D. Taylor . . . has written another winner."
—*The New York Times Book Review*

"A personal, poignant look at a black child's first experience with institutional racism."
—*The New York Times*

THE
FRIENDSHIP

ILLUSTRATED BY MAX GINSBURG

—— and ——
THE
GOLD
CADILLAC

ILLUSTRATED BY MICHAEL HAYS

TWO STORIES BY

MILDRED D. TAYLOR

A YEARLING BOOK

Published by
Bantam Doubleday Dell Books for Young Readers
a division of
Bantam Doubleday Dell Publishing Group, Inc.
1540 Broadway
New York, New York 10036

ISBN: 0-440-41307-9

Reprinted by arrangement with Dial Books for
Young Readers

Printed in the United States of America

April 1996

10   9   8   7   6   5   4   3   2

The
FRIENDSHIP

In memory of my father, the storyteller

"Now don't y'all go touchin' nothin'," Stacey warned as we stepped onto the porch of the Wallace store. Christopher-John, Little Man, and I readily agreed to that. After all, we weren't even supposed to be up here. "And Cassie," he added, "don't you say nothin'."

"Now, boy, what I'm gonna say?" I cried, indignant that he should single me out.

"Just mind my words, hear? Now come on." Stacey started for the door, then stepped back as Jeremy Simms, a blond sad-eyed boy, came out. Looking out from under the big straw hat he was wearing, he glanced somewhat shyly at us, then gave a nod. We took a moment and nodded back. At first I thought Jeremy was going to say something. He looked as if he wanted to, but then he walked on past and went slowly down the steps. We all watched him. He got as far as the corner of the porch and looked back. The boys and I turned and went into the store.

Once inside we stood in the entrance a moment, somewhat hesitant now about being here. At the back counter, two of the storekeepers, Thurston and Dewberry Wallace, were stocking shelves. They glanced over, then paid us no further attention. I didn't much like them. Mama and Papa didn't much like them either. They didn't much like any of the Wallaces and that included Dewberry and Thurston's brother, Kaleb, and their father, John. They said the Wallaces didn't treat our folks right and it was best to stay clear of them. Because of that they didn't come up to this store to shop and we weren't supposed to be coming up here either.

We all knew that. But today as we had walked the red road toward home, Aunt Callie Jackson, who wasn't really our aunt but whom everybody called that because she was so old, had hollered to us from her front porch and said she had the headache bad. She said her nephew Joe was gone off somewhere and she had nobody to send to the store for head medicine. We couldn't say no to her, not to Aunt Callie. So despite Mama's and Papa's warnings about this Wallace place, we had taken it upon ourselves to come anyway. Stacey had said they would understand and after a moment's thought had added that if they didn't he would take the blame and that had settled it. After all, he was twelve with three years on me, so I made no objection about the thing. Christopher-John and Little Man, younger still, nodded agreement and that was that.

"Now mind what I said," Stacey warned us again, then headed for the back counter and the Wallaces. Christopher-John, Little Man, and I remained by the front door looking the store over; it was our first time in the place. The store was small, not nearly as large as it had looked from the outside peeping in. Farm supplies and household and food goods were sparsely displayed on the shelves and counters and the floor space too, while on the walls were plastered posters of a man called Roosevelt. In the center of the store was a potbellied stove, and near it a table and some chairs. But nobody was sitting there. In fact, there were no other customers in the store.

Our eyes roamed over it all with little interest; then we spotted the three large jars of candy on one of the counters. One was filled with lemon drops, another with licorice, and a third with candy canes. Christopher-John, who was seven, round, and had himself a mighty sweet tooth, glanced around at Little Man and me, grinning. Then he walked over to the candy jars for a closer look. There he stood staring at them with a hungry longing even though he knew good and well there would be no candy for him this day. There never was for any of us except at Christmastime. Little Man started to follow him, but then something else caught his eye. Something gleaming and shining. Belt buckles and lockets, cuff links, and tie clips in a glass case. As soon as Little Man saw them, he forgot about the jars of candy and strutted right over. Little Man loved shiny new things.

Not interested in drooling over candy I knew I couldn't have, or shiny new things either, I went on to the back and stood with Stacey. Since the Wallaces were taking their own good time about serving us, I busied myself studying a brand-new 1933 catalog that lay open on the counter. Finally, Dewberry asked what we wanted. Stacey was about to tell him, but before he could, Dewberry's eyes suddenly widened and he slapped the rag he was holding against the counter and hollered, "Get them filthy hands off-a-there!"

Stacey and I turned to see who he was yelling at. So did Christophe·-John. Then we saw Little Man. Excited by the lure of all those shiny new things, Little Man had forgotten Stacey's warning. Standing on tiptoe, he was bracing himself with both hands against the top of the glass counter for a better look inside. Now he glanced around. He found Dewberry's eyes on him and snatched his hands away. He hid them behind his back.

Dewberry, a full-grown man, stared down at Little Man. Little Man, only six, looked up. "Now I'm gonna hafta clean that glass again," snapped Dewberry, "seeing you done put them dirty hands-a yours all over it!"

"My hands ain't dirty," Little Man calmly informed him. He seemed happy that he could set Dewberry's mind to rest if that was all that was bothering him. Little Man pulled his hands from behind his back and inspected them. He turned his hands inward. He turned them outward. Then he held them up for Dewberry to see. "They clean!" he said. "They ain't dirty! They clean!"

Dewberry came from around the corner. "Boy, you disputin' my word? Just look at ya! Skin's black as dirt. Could put seeds on ya and have 'em growin' in no time!"

Thurston Wallace laughed and tossed his brother an ax from one of the shelves. "Best chop them hands off, Dew, they that filthy!"

Little Man's eyes widened at the sight of the ax. He slapped his hands behind himself again and backed away. Stacey hurried over and put an arm around him. Keeping eyes on the Wallaces, he brought Little Man back to stand with us. Thurston and Dewberry laughed.

We got Aunt Callie's head medicine and hurried out. As we reached the steps we ran into Mr. Tom Bee carrying a fishing pole and two strings of fish. Mr. Tom Bee was an elderly, toothless man who had a bit of sharecropping land over on the Granger Plantation. But Mr. Tom Bee didn't do much farming these days.

Instead he spent most of his days fishing. Mr. Tom Bee loved to fish. "Well, now," he said, coming up the steps, "where y'all younguns headed to?"

Stacey nodded toward the crossroads. "Over to Aunt Callie's, then on home."

"Y'all hold on up a minute, I walk with ya. Got a mess-a fish for Aunt Callie. Jus' wants to drop off this here other string and get me some more-a my sardines. I loves fishin' cat, but I keeps me a taste for sardines!" he laughed.

Stacey watched him go into the store, then looked back to the road. There wasn't much to see. There was a lone gas pump in front of the store. There were two red roads that crossed each other, and a dark forest that loomed on the other three corners of the crossroads. That was all, yet Stacey was staring out intensely as if there were more to see. A troubled look was on his face and anger was in his eyes.

"You figure we best head on home?" I asked.

"Reckon we can wait, Mr. Tom Bee don't take too long," he said, then leaned moodily back against the post. I knew his moods and I knew this one had nothing to do with Mr. Tom Bee. So I let him be and sat down on the steps in the shade of the porch trying to escape some of the heat. It was miserably hot. But then it most days was in a Mississippi summer. Christopher-John sat down too, but not Little Man. He remained by the open doors staring into the store. Christopher-John noticed him there and immediately hopped back up again. Always sympathizing with other folks' feelings, he went over to Little Man and tried to comfort him. "Don'tcha worry now, Man," he said, patting his shoulder. "Don'tcha worry! We knows you ain't dirty!"

"That ain't what they said!" shrieked Little Man, his voice revealing the hurt he felt. Little Man took great pride in being clean.

Stacey turned to them. "Man, forget about what they said. You can't pay them no mind."

"But, St-Stacey! They said they could plant seeds on me!" he cried indignantly.

I looked back at him. "Ah, shoot, boy! You know they can't do no such-a thing!"

Skeptically Little Man looked to Stacey for affirmation.

Stacey nodded. "They can do plenty all right, but they can't do nothin' like that."

"But—but, Stacey, th-they s-said they was g-gonna c-cut off my hands. They done s-said

they gonna do that c-cause they... they dirty!"

Stacey said nothing for a moment, then pulled from the post and went over to him. "They was jus' teasin' you, Man," he said softly, "that's all. They was jus' teasin'. Their way of funnin'."

"Wasn't nothin' 'bout it funny to me," I remarked, feeling Little Man's hurt.

Stacey's eyes met mine and I knew he was feeling the same. He brought Little Man back to the steps and the two of them sat down. Little Man, seemingly comforted with Stacey beside him, was silent now. But after a few moments he did a strange thing. He reached down and placed his hand flat to the dirt. He looked at his hand, looked at the dirt, then drew back again. Without a word, he folded his hands tightly together and held them very still in his lap.

I looked at the ground, then at him. "Now what was all that about?"

Little Man looked at me, his eyes deeply troubled. And once again, Stacey said, "Forget it, Man, forget it."

Little Man said nothing, but I could tell he wasn't forgetting anything. I stared down at the dirt. I wasn't forgetting either.

"'Ey, y'all."

We turned. Jeremy Simms was standing at the corner of the porch.

"Boy, I thought you was gone!" I said.

Stacey nudged me to be quiet, but didn't say anything to Jeremy himself. Jeremy bit at his lip, his face reddening. Rubbing one bare foot against the other, he pushed his hands deep into his overall pockets. "C-come up here to wait on my pa and R. W. and Melvin," he explained. "Got a load to pick up. Been waiting a good while now."

Stacey nodded. There wasn't anything to say to that. Jeremy seemed to understand there was nothing to say. A fly buzzed near his face. He brushed it away, looked out at the crossroads, then sat down at the end of the porch and leaned against a post facing us. He pulled one leg up toward his chest and left the other leg dangling over the side of the porch. He glanced at us, looked out at the crossroads, then back at us again. "Y'all . . . y'all been doin' a lotta fishin' here lately?"

Stacey glanced over. "Fish when we can."

"Over on the Rosa Lee?"

Stacey nodded his answer.

"I fish over there sometimes. . . ."

"Most folks do. . . ." said Stacey.

Jeremy was silent a moment as if thinking on what he should say next. "Y'all . . . y'all spect to be goin' fishin' again anyways soon?"

Stacey shook his head. "Cotton time's here. Got too much work to do now for much fishin'."

"Yeah, me too I reckon. . . ."

Jeremy looked away once more and was quiet once more. I watched him, trying to figure him out. The boy was a mighty puzzlement to me, the way he was always talking friendly to us. I didn't understand it. He was white.

Stacey saw me staring and shook his head, letting me know I shouldn't be doing it. So I stopped. After that we all just sat there in the muggy midday heat listening to the sounds of bees and flies and cawing blackbirds and kept our silence. Then we heard voices rising inside the store and turned to look. Mr. Tom Bee, the string of fish and the fishing pole still in his hand, was standing before the counter listening to Dewberry.

"Now look here, old uncle," said Dewberry, "I told you three times my daddy's busy! You tell me what you want or get on outa here. I ain't got all day to fool with you."

Mr. Tom Bee was a slightly built man, and that along with his age made him look somewhat frail, and especially so as he faced the much younger Dewberry. But that look of frailty didn't keep him from speaking his mind. There was a sharp-edged stubbornness to Mr. Tom Bee. His eyes ran over both Dewberry and Thurston and he snapped: "Give me some-a them sardines! Needs me four cans!"

Dewberry leaned across the counter. "You already got plenty-a charges, Tom. You don't need no sardines. Ya stinkin' of fish as it is."

I nudged Stacey. "Now how he know what Mr. Tom Bee need?"

Stacey told me to hush.

"Well, shoot! Mr. Tom Bee been grown more years than 'bout anybody 'round here! He oughta know what he need!"

"Cassie, I said hush!" Stacey glanced back toward the store as if afraid somebody inside might have heard. Then he glanced over at Jeremy, who bit his lower lip and looked away again as if he had heard nothing at all.

Saying nothing else, Stacey looked back at the crossroads. I cut my eyes at him, then sighed. I was tired of always having to watch my mouth whenever white folks were around. Wishing Mr. Tom Bee would get his stuff and come on, I got up and crossed the porch to the doorway. It was then I saw that Christopher-John had eased back inside and was again staring up at the candy jars. I started to tell Stacey that Christopher-John was in the store, then realized Mr. Tom Bee had noticed him too. Seeing Christopher-John standing there, Mr. Tom Bee pointed to the candy and said to Dewberry, "An' you can jus' give me some-a them candy canes there too."

"Don't need no candy canes neither, Tom," decided Dewberry. "Got no teeth to chew 'em with."

Mr. Tom Bee stood his ground. "Y'all can't get them sardines and that candy for me, y'all go get y'alls daddy and let him get it! Where John anyway?" he demanded. "He give me what I ask for, you sorry boys won't!"

Suddenly the store went quiet. I could feel something was wrong. Stacey got up. I looked at him. We both knew this name business was a touchy thing. I didn't really understand why, but it was. White folks took it seriously. Mighty seriously. They took it seriously to call every grown black person straight out by their first

name without placing a "mister" or a "missus" or a "miss" anywhere. White folks, young and old, called Mama and Papa straight out by their first names. They called Big Ma by her first name or they sometimes called her aunty because she was in her sixties now and that was their way of showing her age some respect, though Big Ma said she didn't need that kind of respect. She wasn't *their* aunty. They took seriously too the way we addressed them. All the white grown folks I knew expected to be addressed proper with that "mister" and "missus" sounding loud ahead of their names. No, I didn't understand it. But I understood enough to know Mr. Tom Bee could be in trouble standing up in this store calling Dewberry and Thurston's father John straight out.

Jeremy glanced from the store to us, watching, his lips pressed tight. I could tell he understood the seriousness of names too. Stacey moved toward me. It was then he saw Christopher-John inside the store. He bit his lip nervously, as if trying to decide if he should bring attention to Christopher-John by going in to get him. I think the quiet made him wait.

Dewberry pointed a warning finger at Mr.

Tom Bee. "Old nigger," he said, "don't you never in this life speak to me that way again. And don't you never stand up there with yo' black face and speak of my daddy or any other white man without the proper respect. You might be of a forgetful mind at yo' age, but you forgettin' the wrong thing when you forgettin' who you are. A nigger, nothin' but a nigger. You may be old, Tom, but you ain't too old to teach and you ain't too old to whip!"

My breath caught and I shivered. It was such a little thing, I figured, this thing about a name. I just couldn't understand it. I just couldn't understand it at all.

The back door to the store slammed and a man appeared in the doorway. He was average-built and looked to be somewhere in his fifties. The man was John Wallace, Dewberry and Thurston's father. He looked at Mr. Tom Bee, then motioned to his sons. "I take care-a this," he said.

Mr. Tom Bee grinned. "Well, howdy there, John!" he exclaimed. "Glad ya finally done brought yourself on in here! These here boys-a yours ain't been none too friendly."

John Wallace looked solemnly at Mr. Tom Bee. "What ya want, Tom?"

"Wants me my sardines and some candy there, John."

Dewberry slammed his fist hard upon the counter. "Daddy! How come you to let this old nigger disrespect ya this here way? Just lettin' him stand there and talk to you like he was a white man! He need teachin', Daddy! He need teachin'!"

"Dew's right," said Thurston. "Them old britches done stretched way too big!"

John Wallace wheeled around and fixed hard, unrelenting eyes on his sons. "Y'all hush up and get on to ya business! There's stackin' to be done out back!"

"But, Daddy—"

"I said get!"

For a moment Dewberry and Thurston didn't move. The heat seemed more stifling. The quiet more quiet. John Wallace kept eyes on his sons. Dewberry and Thurston left the store.

As the back door closed behind them Stacey went in and got Christopher-John. Mr. John Wallace took note of him, took note of all of us, and as Stacey and Christopher-John came out he came behind and closed the doors. But he forgot the open windows. He turned back to

Mr. Tom Bee. "Now, Tom," he said, "I done told you before 'bout calling me by my Christian name, it ain't jus' the two of us. It ain't seemly, you here a nigger and me a white man. Now you ain't used to do it. Some folks say it's yo' old age. Say your age is making you forget 'bout way things is. But I say it ain't your age, it's your orneriness."

Mr. Tom Bee squared his shoulders. "An' I done tole you, it ain't seemly t' me to be callin' no white man mister when I done saved his sorry hide when he wasn't hardly no older'n them younguns standin' out yonder! You owes me, John. Ya knows ya owes me too."

John Wallace walked back to the counter. "Ain't necessarily what I'm wanting, but what's gotta be. You just can't keep going 'round callin' me by my first name no more. Folks been taking note. Makes me look bad. Even my boys been questionin' me on why I lets ya do it."

"Then tell 'em, doggonit!"

"I'm losin' face, Tom."

"Now, what you think I care 'bout your face, boy? I done saved your hide more'n one time and I gots me a right t' call you whatsoever I pleases t' call you whensoever I be talkin' t' ya!"

John Wallace sucked in his breath. "Naw, Tom, not no more."

Mr. Tom Bee sucked in his breath too. "You figure the years done made you forget how come you alive an' still breathin'?"

"Figure the years done give me sense 'bout this thing."

"Well, you live long 'nough, maybe the next years gonna give you the sense 'nough t' be grateful. Now put these here sardines on my charges." He glanced over at the candy jars. "An' give me two pennies worth-a them there candy sticks while's you at it."

Mr. Tom Bee stood quietly waiting as if expecting his order to be obeyed, and to our surprise Mr. John Wallace did obey. He reached into the candy jar, pulled out a fistful of candy canes, and handed them to him. Mr. Tom Bee took the candy canes and gave John Wallace a nod. Mr. John Wallace put both hands flat on the counter.

"Tom, mind what I say now. My patience done worn thin 'bout 'mindin' you 'bout what's proper. Next time you come in here, you make sure you address me right, you hear?"

Mr. Tom Bee cackled a laugh and slapped one

string of fish on the counter. "These here for you, John. Knows how much you like catfish, so these here for you!" Then, still chuckling, he picked up his cans of sardines and stuffed them into his pockets, turned his back on John Wallace, and left the store.

As soon as Mr. Tom Bee was outside, he looked down at Christopher-John and said, "How'd y'all younguns like a little bit-a candy?"

"Like it just fine, Mr. Tom Bee!" spoke up Christopher-John.

Mr. Tom Bee laughed and handed him a stick, then presented one each to Stacey, Little Man, and me. Stacey, Christopher-John, and I were mighty thankful, but Little Man only looked joylessly at his candy cane and stuck it into his shirt pocket.

"What's this?" asked Mr. Tom Bee. "What's this? Ain't ya gonna eat that candy cane, boy?"

Little Man shook his head.

"Well, why not? Mighty good!"

"Don't want they ole candy canes! They said I was dirty! I ain't dirty, Mr. Tom Bee!"

Mr. Tom Bee put his hands on his hips and laughed. "Lord have mercy! Course ya ain't,

boy! Don't you know them Wallace boys ain't got no more good sense'n a wall-eyed mule! Last thing in the world ya wantin' to be doin' is listenin' to anything they gotta say! They say somethin's red, ya best be figurin' it's green. They say somethin' dirty, ya gotta know it's clean. Shuckies, Little Man! You got more sense with them six years a your'n than them two boys ever gonna see. Don't ya never pay them no mind!"

Little Man thought on that, looked around at Stacey, who nodded his agreement with Mr. Tom Bee, then took the candy cane from his pocket and gave it a listless lick.

Then Mr. Tom Bee noticed Jeremy and snapped, "You the kinda boy keep hold to yo' promises?"

Jeremy, who seemed taken aback by the question, nodded mutely.

At that, Mr. Tom Bee pulled forth another candy cane and held it out to him. The boys and I waited, wondering if Jeremy would take it. Jeremy seemed to be wondering if he should. He hesitated, looked around as if fearful someone other than we would see, and took it. He didn't actually say thank you to Mr. Tom Bee, but then the nod he gave and his eyes did. I had a feeling Jeremy didn't see much penny candy either.

As Mr. Tom Bee, the boys, and I started down the road, Jeremy called after us. "Stacey! May— maybe one-a these here days, maybe I go fishin' with y'all. . . ."

"Yeah. . . ." Stacey replied. "Yeah, one-a these days, maybe so. . . ."

We headed on toward Aunt Callie's. Stacey sucked thoughtfully at his candy stick, then looked up at Mr. Tom Bee. "Mr. Tom Bee, something I been thinkin' on."

"What's that, boy?"

"'Bout how come you to call Mr. Wallace plain-out by his first name. I mean you don't call him mister or nothin'." He paused. "Don't know nobody else to do, nobody colored I mean. Fact to business, don't know nobody colored call a white man straight to his face by his first name."

Mr. Tom Bee laughed. "He call me straight-out Tom 'thout no mister, don't he now?"

Stacey nodded. "Yes, sir, that's a fact, but that's the way white folks do. Papa say white folks set an awful store 'bout names and such. He say they get awful riled 'bout them names too. Say they can do some terrible things when they get riled. Say anybody call a white man straight out by his name just lookin' for trouble."

"Well, that's sho the truth all right," agreed Mr. Tom Bee. "But shuckies! I ain't studyin' they foolish way-a things and I ain't gonna be callin' that John Wallace no mister neither! He done promised me long time ago I could call him straight out by his name long's I lived an' I aims to see he holds to his promises." He paused, then added, "'Sides, we used t' be friends."

"Friends?" said Stacey as if he didn't understand the word.

"That's right. Me and that John Wallace, we goes way back. Long ways back. Why, shuckies! I done saved that boy's life."

We all looked up from our candy canes.

"That's right!" he said with an emphatic nod. "Sho did! That John Wallace wasn't no more'n fifteen when I come along the road one day and found him sinkin' in swampland and pulled him out. Asked him what his name was. He said, call me John. So's that what I called him, jus' that. John. But that there was only the first time I done saved his life.

"No sooner'n I done got him outa that swampland, I come t' find out he was burnin' up with fever, so's I doctored him. Ain't never laid eyes on the boy before, but I doctored him anyways. Doctored him till I got him well. Turned out the boy ain't had no family round here. Said he was coming up from down Biloxi way when he landed hisself in that swamp. Anyways, I let him stay on with me till he got hisself strong. Let him stay on long's he wanted and that was for quite some while, till the white folks round started meddlin' 'bout a white boy stayin' wit' me. I done took care-a John Wallace like a daddy woulda and long's he stayed with me, he minded what I said and was right respectful."

Stacey shook his head as if finding that hard to believe.

Mr. Tom Bee saw the disbelief and assured him it was so. "That's right! Right respectful, and all that time, I been callin' him John. Jus' that. John. Well, come the day John Wallace tole me he was goin' up to Vicksburg to look for a job an' I said to him I figured next time I see him, I 'spected I'd most likely hafta be callin' him *Mister* John. And he told me things wasn't never gonna be that way. He says to me, I'm John t' you now, gonna always be John t' ya, cause you

been like a daddy t' me an' I couldn't never 'spect my daddy to go callin' me mister. He done promised me that. Promised me he wasn't never gonna forget what I done for him. Said he was gonna always owe me. But then he come back down in here some years later to set up that store and things had done changed. He 'spected all the colored folks to call him 'Mister' John, and that there done included ole Tom Bee."

"Owww," I said, "Mr. John Wallace done broke his word!"

"He sho done that all right! Now I been thinkin' here lately maybe it's time I makes him keep his word. I figures I'm close 'nough to meetin' my Maker, it don't much matter he like it or not. I ain't studyin' that boy!"

I took a lick of candy. "Well, Big Ma—she say you gonna get yourself in a whole lotta trouble, Mr. Tom Bee. She say all them years on you done made you go foolish—"

"Cassie!" Stacey rebuked me with a hard look.

I gave him a look right back. "Well, she did!" Not only had Big Ma said it, but plenty of other folks had too. They said Mr. Tom Bee had just all of a sudden up and started calling Mr. Wallace

John. He had started after years of addressing John Wallace like the white folks expected him to do. Most folks figured the only reason for him to do a fool thing like that was because he had gone forgetful, that his advancing years were making him think it was a long time back when John Wallace was still a boy. I told it all. "Said you just full of foolishness callin' that man by his name that way!"

Mr. Tom Bee stopped right in the middle of the road, slapped his thighs, and let go a rip of a laugh. "Well, ya know somethin', Cassie? Maybe yo' grandmama's right! Jus' maybe she sho is! Maybe I done gone foolish! Jus' maybe I has!"

He laughed so hard standing there, I thought he was going to cry. But then after a few moments he started walking again and the boys and I got right into step. Still chuckling, Mr. Tom Bee said he couldn't rightly say he hadn't been called foolish before. In fact, he said, he'd been called foolish more times than he wanted to remember. Then he began to tell us about one of those times, and the boys and I listened eagerly. We loved to hear Mr. Tom Bee tell his stories. With all his years, he had plenty of stories to tell too. He had seen the slavery days and he had seen the war that ended slavery. He had seen Confederate soldiers and he had seen Yankee soldiers. He had seen a lot of things over the years and he said he'd forgotten just about as much as he remembered. But as we walked the road listening to him I for one was mighty glad he had remembered as much as he had.

We reached Aunt Callie's, gave her the head medicine and the fish, then headed back toward home. Mr. Tom Bee was still with us. He lived over our way. To get home we had to pass the Wallace store again. When we reached the cross-roads, Mr. Tom Bee said, "Y'all wait on up jus' another minute here. Done forgot my tobaccie." A truck and a wagon were now in front of the store. Mr. Tom Bee took note of them and stepped onto the porch.

Jeremy Simms was still sitting on the porch, but he didn't say anything to us this time. He nodded slightly, that was all. I noticed he wasn't sucking on his candy cane; I could see it sticking out of his pocket. He bit his lip and looked around uneasily. We didn't say anything to him either. We just stood there wanting to get on home. It was getting late.

Mr. Tom Bee entered the store. "'Ey there, John!" he called. "Give me some-a that chewin' tobaccie! Forgot to get it I was in before."

The boys and I, standing by the gas pump, looked into the store. So did Jeremy. His father, Mr. Charlie Simms, was in there now, sitting at the table by the stove along with his older teenage brothers, R.W. and Melvin. Dewberry and Thurston Wallace were there also and two white men we didn't know. They all turned their eyes on Mr. Tom Bee. Dewberry and Thurston glanced at their father, and then Mr. Charlie Simms spoke up. "Old nigger," he said, "who you think you talkin' to?"

Mr. Tom Bee wet his lips. "Jus' . . . jus' come for my tobaccie."

Mr. John Wallace glanced at the men, then, his jaw hardening, set eyes on Mr. Tom Bee. "You bes' get on outa here, Tom."

Mr. Tom Bee looked around at the men. His back straightened with that old, sharp-edged stubbornness. "Well, I sho do that, John," he said, "soon's I get me my tobaccie."

Mr. Simms jumped up from the table. "John Wallace! You jus' gonna let this here old nigger talk t' ya this-a way? You gon' let him do that?"

Suddenly Stacey bounded up the steps to the store entrance. "We—we waitin' on ya, Mr. Tom Bee!" he cried shrilly. "We waitin'! Come on, Mr. Tom Bee! Come on!"

Mr. Tom Bee looked over at him. He took a moment, then he nodded and I thought he was going to come on out. But instead he said, "Be right wit' ya, boy . . . soon's I get me my tobaccie." Then he turned again and faced John Wallace. "You—you gonna give me that tobaccie, John?"

Dewberry pulled from the counter. "Daddy! You don't shut this old nigger up, I'm gonna do it for ya!"

Mr. John Wallace turned a mean look on his son and the look was enough to silence him. Then he looked around the room at Mr. Simms, at R.W. and Melvin, at Thurston, at the two other white men gathered there. The store and all around it was plunged into silence.

Mr. Tom Bee glanced nervously at the men, but he didn't stop. He seemed bent on carrying this thing through. "Well?" he asked of John Wallace. "I'm gonna get me that tobaccie?"

Silently John Wallace reached back to a shelf and got the tobacco. He placed it on the counter.

Mr. Simms exploded. "What kind-a white man

are ya, John Wallace, ya don't shut his black mouth? What kind-a white man?"

Mr. Tom Bee looked at Mr. Simms and the others, then went and picked up the tobacco. "Thank ya, John," he said. "Jus' put it on my charges here, John. Just' put it on my charges." He glanced again at the men and started out. He got as far as the steps. The boys and I turned to go. Then we heard the click. The explosion of a shotgun followed and Mr. Tom Bee tumbled down the steps, his right leg ripped open by the blast.

The boys and I stood stunned, just staring at Mr. Tom Bee at first, not knowing what to do. Stacey started toward him, but Mr. Tom Bee waved him back. "Get 'way from me, boy! Get 'way! Stacey, get them younguns back, 'way from me!" Stacey looked into the store, at the shotgun, and herded us across the road.

The white men came out and sniggered. Mr. John Wallace, carrying the shotgun, came out onto the porch too. He stood there, his face solemn, and said, "You made me do that, Tom. I coulda killed ya, but I ain't wantin' to kill ya 'cause ya done saved my life an' I'm a Christian man so I ain't forgetting that. But this here disrespectin' me gotta stop and I means to stop it now. You gotta keep in mind you ain't nothin' but a nigger. You gonna learn to watch yo' mouth. You gonna learn to address me proper. You hear me, Tom?"

Mr. Tom Bee sat in silence staring at the bloody leg.

"Tom, ya hear me?"

Now, slowly, Mr. Tom Bee raised his head and looked up at John Wallace. "Oh, yeah, I hears ya all right. I hears ya. But let me tell you somethin', John. Ya was John t' me when I saved your sorry life and you give me your word you was always gonna be John t' me long as I lived. So's ya might's well go 'head and kill me cause that's what ya gon' be, John. Ya hear me, John? Till the judgment day. Till the earth opens itself up and the fires-a hell come takes yo' ungrateful soul! Ya hear me, John? Ya hear me? *John! John! John!* Till the judgment day! *John!*"

With that he raised himself to one elbow and began to drag himself down the road. The boys and I, candy canes in hand, stood motionless. We watched Mr. John Wallace to see if he would raise the shotgun again. Jeremy, the candy cane

in his pocket, watched too. We all waited for the second click of the shotgun. But only the cries of Mr. Tom Bee as he inched his way along the road ripped the silence. *"John! John! John!"* he cried over and over again. "Ya hear me, John? Till the judgment day! John! *John! JOHN!"*

There was no other sound.

Author's Note

I was born in the South but I didn't grow up there. In fact, I was only three months old when my parents took my sister and me to live in the North. Over the years of my childhood I came to know the South through the yearly trips my family took to Mississippi and through the stories told whenever the family gathered, both in the North and in the South. Through the stories I learned a history about my family going back to the days of slavery. Through the stories I learned a history not then taught in history books, a history about the often tragic lives of Black people living in a segregated land. My father told many of the stories. Some of the stories he had been told when he was a boy. Some of the stories he actually lived himself. *The Friendship* is based on one of those stories.

The
GOLD CADILLAC

To Mother-Dear,
who has always been there for all of us
with her love and strength and understanding

My sister and I were playing out on the front lawn when the gold Cadillac rolled up and my father stepped from behind the wheel. We ran to him, our eyes filled with wonder. "Daddy, whose Cadillac?" I asked.

And Wilma demanded, "Where's our Mercury?"

My father grinned. "Go get your mother and I'll tell you all about it."

"Is it ours?" I cried. "Daddy, is it ours?"

"Get your mother!" he laughed. "And tell her to hurry!" Wilma and I ran off to obey as Mr. Pondexter next door came from his house to see

what this new Cadillac was all about. We threw open the front door, ran through the downstairs front parlor and straight through the house to the kitchen where my mother was cooking and one of my aunts was helping her. "Come on, Mother-Dear!" we cried together. "Daddy say come on out and see this new car!"

"What?" said my mother, her face showing her surprise. "What're you talking about?"

"A Cadillac!" I cried.

"He said hurry up!" relayed Wilma.

And then we took off again, up the back stairs to the second floor of the duplex. Running down the hall, we banged on all the apartment doors. My uncles and their wives stepped to the doors. It was good it was a Saturday morning. Everybody was home.

"We got us a Cadillac! We got us a Cadillac!" Wilma and I proclaimed in unison. We had decided that the Cadillac had to be ours if our father was driving it and holding on to the keys. "Come on see!" Then we raced on, through the upstairs sunroom, down the front steps, through the downstairs sunroom, and out to the Cadillac. Mr. Pondexter was still there. Mr. LeRoy and Mr. Courtland from down the street were there too and all were admiring the Cadillac as my father stood proudly by, pointing out the various features.

"Brand-new 1950 Coupe deVille!" I heard one of the men saying.

"Just off the showroom floor!" my father said. "I just couldn't resist it."

My sister and I eased up to the car and peeked in. It was all gold inside. Gold leather seats. Gold carpeting. Gold dashboard. It was like no car we had owned before. It looked like a car for rich folks.

"Daddy, are we rich?" I asked. My father laughed.

"Daddy, it's ours, isn't it?" asked Wilma, who was older and more practical than I. She didn't intend to give her heart too quickly to something that wasn't hers.

"You like it?"

"Oh, Daddy, yes!"

He looked at me. "What 'bout you, 'lois?"

"Yes, sir!"

My father laughed again. "Then I expect I can't much disappoint my girls, can I? It's ours all right!"

Wilma and I hugged our father with our joy.

My uncles came from the house and my aunts, carrying their babies, came out too. Everybody surrounded the car and owwed and ahhed. Nobody could believe it.

Then my mother came out.

Everybody stood back grinning as she approached the car. There was no smile on her face. We all waited for her to speak. She stared at the car, then looked at my father, standing there as proud as he could be. Finally she said, "You didn't buy this car, did you, Wilbert?"

"Gotta admit I did. Couldn't resist it."

"But . . . but what about our Mercury? It was perfectly good!"

"Don't you like the Cadillac, Dee?"

"That Mercury wasn't even a year old!"

My father nodded. "And I'm sure whoever buys it is going to get themselves a good car. But we've got ourselves a better one. Now stop frowning, honey, and let's take ourselves a ride in our brand-new Cadillac!"

My mother shook her head. "I've got food on the stove," she said and turning away walked back to the house.

There was an awkward silence and then my father said, "You know Dee never did much like

surprises. Guess this here Cadillac was a bit too much for her. I best go smooth things out with her."

Everybody watched as he went after my mother. But when he came back, he was alone.

"Well, what she say?" asked one of my uncles.

My father shrugged and smiled. "Told me I bought this Cadillac alone, I could just ride in it alone."

Another uncle laughed. "Uh-oh! Guess she told you!"

"Oh, she'll come around," said one of my aunts. "Any woman would be proud to ride in this car."

"That's what I'm banking on," said my father as he went around to the street side of the car and opened the door. "All right! Who's for a ride?"

"We are!" Wilma and I cried.

All three of my uncles and one of my aunts, still holding her baby, and Mr. Pondexter climbed in with us and we took off for the first ride in the gold Cadillac. It was a glorious ride and we drove all through the city of Toledo. We rode past the church and past the school. We rode through Ottawa Hills where the rich folks lived and on into Walbridge Park and past the zoo, then along the Maumee River. But none us had had enough of the car so my father put the car on the road and we drove all the way to Detroit. We had plenty of family there and everybody was just as pleased as could be about the Cadillac. My father told our Detroit relatives that he was in the doghouse with my mother about buying the Cadillac. My uncles told them she wouldn't ride in the car. All the Detroit family thought that was funny and everybody, including my father, laughed about it and said my mother would come around.

It was early evening by the time we got back home, and I could see from my mother's face she had not come around. She was angry now not only about the car, but that we had been gone so long. I didn't understand that, since my father had called her as soon as we reached Detroit to let her know where we were. I had heard him myself. I didn't understand either why she did not like that fine Cadillac and thought she was being terribly disagreeable with my father. That night as she tucked Wilma and me in bed I told her that too.

"Is this your business?" she asked.

"Well, I just think you ought to be nice to Daddy. I think you ought to ride in that car with him! It'd sure make him happy."

"I think you ought to go to sleep," she said and turned out the light.

Later I heard her arguing with my father. "We're supposed to be saving for a house!" she said.

"We've already got a house!" said my father.

"But you said you wanted a house in a better neighborhood. I thought that's what we both said!"

"I haven't changed my mind."

"Well, you have a mighty funny way of saving for it, then. Your brothers are saving for houses of their own and you don't see them out buying new cars every year!"

"We'll still get the house, Dee. That's a promise!"

"Not with new Cadillacs we won't!" said my mother and then she said a very loud good night and all was quiet.

The next day was Sunday and everybody figured that my mother would be sure to give in and ride in the Cadillac. After all, the family always went to church together on Sunday. But she didn't give in. What was worse she wouldn't let Wilma and me ride in the Cadillac either. She took us each by the hand, walked past the Cadillac where my father stood waiting and headed on toward the church, three blocks away. I was really mad at her now. I had been looking forward to driving up to the church in that gold Cadillac and having everybody see.

On most Sunday afternoons during the summertime, my mother, my father, Wilma, and I would go for a ride. Sometimes we just rode around the city and visited friends and family. Sometimes we made short trips over to Chicago or Peoria or Detroit to see relatives there or to Cleveland where we had relatives too, but we could also see the Cleveland Indians play. Sometimes we joined our aunts and uncles and drove in a caravan out to the park or to the beach. At the park or the beach Wilma and I would run and play. My mother and my aunts would spread a picnic and my father and my uncles would shine their cars.

But on this Sunday afternoon my mother refused to ride anywhere. She told Wilma and me that we could go. So we left her alone in the big, empty house, and the family cars, led by the gold Cadillac, headed for the park. For a while I played and had a good time, but then I stopped playing and went to sit with my father. Despite his laughter he seemed sad to me. I think he was missing my mother as much as I was.

That evening my father took my mother to dinner down at the corner café. They walked. Wilma and I stayed at the house chasing fireflies in the backyard. My aunts and uncles sat in the yard and on the porch, talking and laughing about the day and watching us. It was a soft summer's evening, the kind that came every day and was expected. The smell of charcoal and of barbecue drifting from up the block, the sound of laughter and music and talk drifting from yard to yard were all a part of it. Soon one of my uncles joined Wilma and me in our chase of fireflies and when my mother and father came home we were at it still. My mother and father watched us for awhile, while everybody else watched them to see if my father would take out the Cadillac and if my mother would slide in beside him to take a ride. But it soon became evident that the dinner had not changed my mother's mind. She still refused to ride in the Cadillac. I just couldn't understand her objection to it.

Though my mother didn't like the Cadillac, everybody else in the neighborhood certainly did. That meant quite a few folks too, since we lived on a very busy block. On one corner was a grocery store, a cleaner's, and a gas station. Across the street was a beauty shop and a fish market, and down the street was a bar, another grocery store, the Dixie Theater, the café, and a drugstore. There were always people strolling to or from one of these places and because our house was right in the middle of the block just about everybody had to pass our house and the gold Cadillac. Sometimes people took in the Cadillac as they walked, their heads turning for a longer look as they passed. Then there were people who just outright stopped and took a good look before continuing on their way. I was proud to say that car belonged to my family. I felt mighty important as people called to me as I ran down the street. "'Ey, 'lois! How's that Cadillac, girl? Riding fine?" I told my mother how much everybody liked that car. She was not impressed and made no comment.

Since just about everybody on the block knew everybody else, most folks knew that my mother wouldn't ride in the Cadillac. Because of that, my father took a lot of good-natured kidding from the men. My mother got kidded too as the women said if she didn't ride in that car, maybe some other woman would. And everybody laughed about it and began to bet on who would give in first, my mother or my father. But then my father said he was going to drive the car south into Mississippi to visit my grandparents and everybody stopped laughing.

My uncles stopped.

So did my aunts.

Everybody.

"Look here, Wilbert," said one of my uncles, "it's too dangerous. It's like putting a loaded gun to your head."

"I paid good money for that car," said my father. "That gives me a right to drive it where I please. Even down to Mississippi."

My uncles argued with him and tried to talk him out of driving the car south. So did my aunts and so did the neighbors, Mr. LeRoy, Mr. Courtland, and Mr. Pondexter. They said it was a dangerous thing, a mighty dangerous thing, for a black man to drive an expensive car into the rural South.

"Not much those folks hate more'n to see a

northern Negro coming down there in a fine car," said Mr. Pondexter. "They see those Ohio license plates, they'll figure you coming down uppity, trying to lord your fine car over them!"

I listened, but I didn't understand. I didn't understand why they didn't want my father to drive that car south. It was his.

"Listen to Pondexter, Wilbert!" cried another uncle. "We might've fought a war to free people overseas, but we're not free here! Man, those white folks down south'll lynch you soon's look at you. You know that!"

Wilma and I looked at each other. Neither one of us knew what *lynch* meant, but the word sent a shiver through us. We held each other's hand.

My father was silent, then he said: "All my life I've had to be heedful of what white folks thought. Well, I'm tired of that. I worked hard for everything I got. Got it honest, too. Now I got that Cadillac because I liked it and because it meant something to me that somebody like me from Mississippi could go and buy it. It's my car, I paid for it, and I'm driving it south."

My mother, who had said nothing through all this, now stood. "Then the girls and I'll be going too," she said.

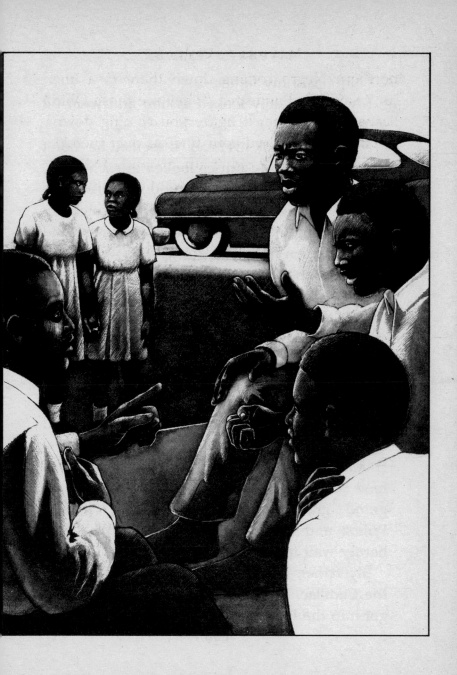

"No!" said my father.

My mother only looked at him and went off to the kitchen.

My father shook his head. It seemed he didn't want us to go. My uncles looked at each other, then at my father. "You set on doing this, we'll all go," they said. "That way we can watch out for each other." My father took a moment and nodded. Then my aunts got up and went off to their kitchens too.

All the next day my aunts and my mother cooked and the house was filled with delicious smells. They fried chicken and baked hams and cakes and sweet potato pies and mixed potato salad. They filled jugs with water and punch and coffee. Then they packed everything in huge picnic baskets along with bread and boiled eggs, oranges and apples, plates and napkins, spoons and forks and cups. They placed all that food on the back seats of the cars. It was like a grand, grand picnic we were going on, and Wilma and I were mighty excited. We could hardly wait to start.

My father, my mother, Wilma, and I got into the Cadillac. My uncles, my aunts, my cousins got into the Ford, the Buick, and the Chevrolet, and we rolled off in our caravan headed south. Though my mother was finally riding in the Cadillac, she had no praise for it. In fact, she said nothing about it at all. She still seemed upset and since she still seemed to feel the same about the car, I wondered why she had insisted upon making this trip with my father.

We left the city of Toledo behind, drove through Bowling Green and down through the Ohio countryside of farms and small towns, through Dayton and Cincinnati, and across the Ohio River into Kentucky. On the other side of the river my father stopped the car and looked back at Wilma and me and said, "Now from here on, whenever we stop and there're white people around, I don't want either one of you to say a word. *Not one word!* Your mother and I'll do all the talking. That understood?"

"Yes, sir," Wilma and I both said, though we didn't truly understand why.

My father nodded, looked at my mother and started the car again. We rolled on, down Highway 25 and through the bluegrass hills of Kentucky. Soon we began to see signs. Signs that read: WHITE ONLY, COLORED NOT ALLOWED. Hours later, we left the Bluegrass State and crossed

into Tennessee. Now we saw even more of the signs saying: WHITE ONLY, COLORED NOT ALLOWED. We saw the signs above water fountains and in restaurant windows. We saw them in ice cream parlors and at hamburger stands. We saw them in front of hotels and motels, and on the rest-room doors of filling stations. I didn't like the signs. I felt as if I were in a foreign land.

I couldn't understand why the signs were there and I asked my father what the signs meant. He said they meant we couldn't drink from the water fountains. He said they meant we couldn't stop to sleep in the motels. He said they meant we couldn't stop to eat in the restau-rants. I looked at the grand picnic basket I had been enjoying so much. Now I understood why my mother had packed it. Suddenly the picnic did not seem so grand.

Finally we reached Memphis. We got there at a bad time. Traffic was heavy and we got separated from the rest of the family. We tried to find them but it was no use. We had to go on alone. We reached the Mississippi state line and soon after we heard a police siren. A police car came up behind us. My father slowed the Cadillac, then stopped. Two white policemen got out of their car. They eyeballed the Cadillac and told my father to get out.

"Whose car is this, boy?" they asked.

I saw anger in my father's eyes. "It's mine," he said.

"You're a liar," said one of the policemen. "You stole this car."

"Turn around, put your hands on top of that car and spread eagle," said the other policeman.

My father did as he was told. They searched him and I didn't understand why. I didn't understand either why they had called my father a liar and didn't believe that the Cadillac was his. I wanted to ask but I remembered my father's warning not to say a word and I obeyed that warning.

The policeman told my father to get in the back of the police car. My father did. One policeman got back into the police car. The other policeman slid behind the wheel of our Cadillac. The police car started off. The Cadillac followed. Wilma and I looked at each other and at our mother. We didn't know what to think. We were scared.

The Cadillac followed the police car into a small town and stopped in front of the police

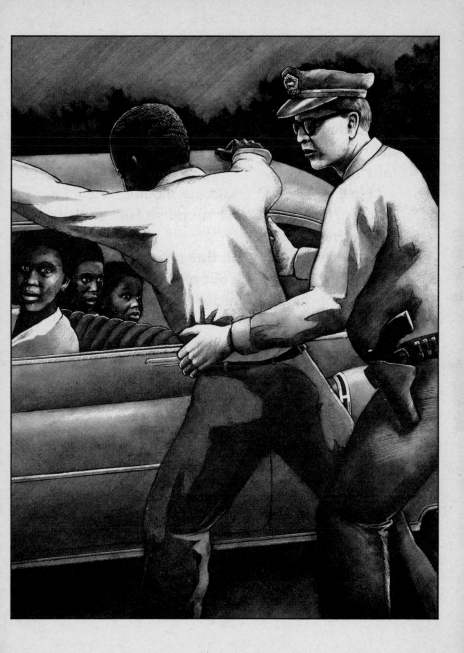

station. The policeman stepped out of our Cadillac and took the keys. The other policeman took my father into the police station.

"Mother-Dear!" Wilma and I cried. "What're they going to do to our daddy? They going to hurt him?"

"He'll be all right," said my mother. "He'll be all right." But she didn't sound so sure of that. She seemed worried.

We waited. More than three hours we waited. Finally my father came out of the police station. We had lots of questions to ask him. He said the police had given him a ticket for speeding and locked him up. But then the judge had come. My father had paid the ticket and they had let him go.

He started the Cadillac and drove slowly out of the town, below the speed limit. The police car followed us. People standing on steps and sitting on porches and in front of stores stared at us as we passed. Finally we were out of the town. The police car still followed. Dusk was falling. The night grew black and finally the police car turned around and left us.

We drove and drove. But my father was tired now and my grandparents' farm was still far away. My father said he had to get some sleep and since my mother didn't drive, he pulled into a grove of trees at the side of the road and stopped.

"I'll keep watch," said my mother.

"Wake me if you see anybody," said my father.

"Just rest," said my mother.

So my father slept. But that bothered me. I needed him awake. I was afraid of the dark and of the woods and of whatever lurked there. My father was the one who kept us safe, he and my uncles. But already the police had taken my father away from us once today and my uncles were lost.

"Go to sleep, baby," said my mother. "Go to sleep."

But I was afraid to sleep until my father woke. I had to help my mother keep watch. I figured I had to help protect us too, in case the police came back and tried to take my father away again. There was a long, sharp knife in the picnic basket and I took hold of it, clutching it tightly in my hand. Ready to strike, I sat there in the back of the car, eyes wide, searching the blackness outside the Cadillac. Wilma, for a while, searched the night too, then she fell

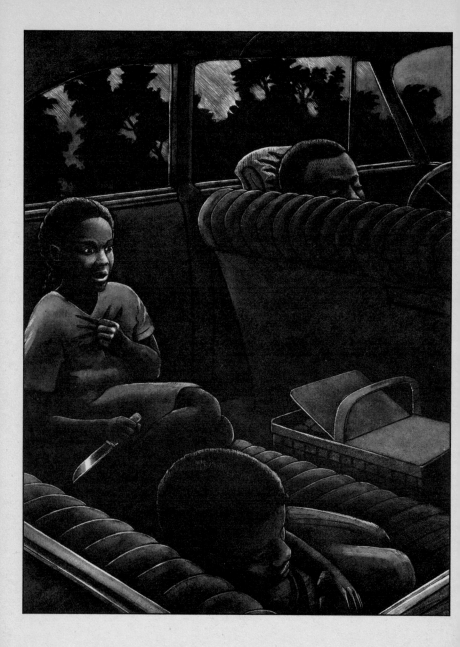

asleep. I didn't want to sleep, but soon I found I couldn't help myself as an unwelcome drowsiness came over me. I had an uneasy sleep and when I woke it was dawn and my father was gently shaking me. I woke with a start and my hand went up, but the knife wasn't there. My mother had it.

My father took my hand. "Why were you holding the knife, 'lois?" he asked.

I looked at him and at my mother. "I—I was scared," I said.

My father was thoughtful. "No need to be scared now, sugar," he said. "Daddy's here and so is Mother-Dear." Then after a glance at my mother, he got out of the car, walked to the road, looked down it one way, then the other. When he came back and started the motor, he turned the Cadillac north, not south.

"What're you doing?" asked my mother.

"Heading back to Memphis," said my father. "Cousin Halton's there. We'll leave the Cadillac and get his car. Driving this car any farther south with you and the girls in the car, it's just not worth the risk."

And so that's what we did. Instead of driving through Mississippi in golden splendor, we traveled its streets and roads and highways in Cousin Halton's solid, yet not so splendid, four-year-old Chevy. When we reached my grandparents' farm, my uncles and aunts were already there. Everybody was glad to see us. They had been worried. They asked about the Cadillac. My father told them what had happened, and they nodded and said he had done the best thing.

We stayed one week in Mississippi. During that week I often saw my father, looking deep in thought, walk off alone across the family land. I saw my mother watching him. One day I ran after my father, took his hand, and walked the land with him. I asked him all the questions that were on my mind. I asked him why the policemen had treated him the way they had and why people didn't want us to eat in the restaurants or drink from the water fountains or sleep in the hotels. I told him I just didn't understand all that.

My father looked at me and said that it all was a difficult thing to understand and he didn't really understand it himself. He said it all had to do with the fact that black people had once been forced to be slaves. He said it had to do with our skins being colored. He said it had to do with stupidity and ignorance. He said it had to do with the law, the law that said we could be treated like this here in the South. And for that matter, he added, any other place in these United States where folks thought the same as so many folks did here in the South. But he also said, "I'm hoping one day though we can drive that long road down here and there won't be any signs. I'm hoping one day the police won't stop us just because of the color of our skins and we're riding in a gold Cadillac with northern plates."

When the week ended, we said a sad good-bye to my grandparents and all the Mississippi family and headed in a caravan back toward Memphis. In Memphis we returned Cousin Halton's car and got our Cadillac. Once we were home my father put the Cadillac in the garage and didn't drive it. I didn't hear my mother say any more about the Cadillac. I didn't hear my father speak of it either.

Some days passed and then on a bright Saturday afternoon while Wilma and I were playing

in the backyard, I saw my father go into the garage. He opened the garage door wide so the sunshine streamed in, and began to shine the Cadillac. I saw my mother at the kitchen window staring out across the yard at my father. For a long time, she stood there watching my father shine his car. Then she came out and crossed the yard to the garage and I heard her say, "Wilbert, you keep the car."

He looked at her as if he had not heard.

"You keep it," she repeated and turned and walked back to the house.

My father watched her until the back door had shut behind her. Then he went on shining the car and soon began to sing. About an hour later he got into the car and drove away. That evening when he came back he was walking. The Cadillac was nowhere in sight.

"Daddy, where's our new Cadillac?" I demanded to know. So did Wilma.

He smiled and put his hand on my head. "Sold it," he said as my mother came into the room.

"But how come?" I asked. "We poor now?"

"No, sugar. We've got more money towards

our new house now and we're all together. I figure that makes us about the richest folks in the world." He smiled at my mother and she smiled too and came into his arms.

After that we drove around in an old 1930s Model A Ford my father had. He said he'd factory-ordered us another Mercury, this time with my mother's approval. Despite that, most folks on the block figured we had fallen on hard times after such a splashy showing of good times and some folks even laughed at us as the Ford rattled around the city. I must admit that at first I was pretty much embarrassed to be riding around in that old Ford after the splendor of the Cadillac. But my father said to hold my head high. We and the family knew the truth. As fine as the Cadillac had been, he said, it had pulled us apart for awhile. Now, as ragged and noisy as that old Ford was, we all rode in it together and we were a family again. So I held my head high.

Still though, I thought often of that Cadillac. We had had the Cadillac only a little more than a month, but I wouldn't soon forget its splendor or how I'd felt riding around inside it. I wouldn't

soon forget either the ride we had taken south in it. I wouldn't soon forget the signs, the policemen, or my fear. I would remember that ride and the gold Cadillac all my life.

Author's Note

For a few years when I was a child, I lived in a big house on a busy street with my mother, my father, my sister, and many aunts and uncles and cousins. We were originally a Mississippi family who had migrated to the industrial North during and after World War II. My father was the first of the family to go to the North and that was when I was only three weeks old. When I was three months old, my mother, my older sister, and I followed. A year after our arrival, my parents bought the big house on the busy street. During the next nine years, aunts and uncles and cousins from both sides of the family arrived yearly from Mississippi and stayed in that big house with us until they had earned enough to rent another place or buy houses of their own.

I loved those years.

There were always cousins to play with. There was always an aunt or an uncle to talk to when my parents were busy, and there seemed always to be fun things to do and plenty of people to do them with. On the weekends the whole houseful of family often did things together. Because my father, my uncles, and my older male cousins all loved cars, we often rode in a caravan out to the park where the men would park their cars in a long, impressive row and shine them in the shade of the trees while the women spread a picnic and chatted, and my sister, younger cousins, and I ran and played. Sometimes we traveled to nearby cities to see other family members or to watch a baseball game. And sometimes we took even longer trips, down country highways into that land called the South.

I have many good memories of those years, including the year my father brought home a brand-new Cadillac. I also have memories of those years that long troubled me. I have woven some of those memories into this story of fiction called *The Gold Cadillac*.

MILDRED D. TAYLOR introduced Cassie Logan in *Song of the Trees* and then continued her story with *Roll of Thunder, Hear My Cry, Let the Circle Be Unbroken*, and now *The Friendship*. *The Gold Cadillac* is a story from Ms. Taylor's own life. Among the numerous honors her books have received are the Newbery Medal, the Coretta Scott King Award, selection as a *New York Times* Outstanding Book of the Year, and a nomination for the American Book Award.

Mildred D. Taylor was born in Jackson, Mississippi, and grew up in Toledo, Ohio. After two years with the Peace Corps, Ms. Taylor enrolled at the School of Journalism of the University of Colorado, where she worked with university officials and fellow students in structuring a Black Studies program at the university. She now lives in Colorado.

MAX GINSBURG, illustrator of *The Friendship*, has exhibited his paintings in many one-man shows, and has also created book covers and magazine illustrations. He has received a number of awards, including the Gold Medal from the Society of Illustrators. In addition to painting, he also teaches art in New York City, where he now lives.

MICHAEL HAYS, illustrator of *The Gold Cadillac*, has worked in graphic design, book illustration, and computer graphics. He illustrated *Abiyoyo* by Pete Seeger. Mr. Hays lives in Chicago.